To my daughter Mari Montejo, with her father's immense love. So that she can live and feel the magic in her parents' and ancestors' Maya traditions. — VM

To Irene, joy itself. — RY

Groundwood Books / House of Anansi Press
720 Bathurst Street, Suite 500, Toronto, Ontario M5S 2R4
Distributed in the USA by Publishers Group West
1700 Fourth Street, Berkeley, CA 94710

Library and Archives Canada Cataloging in Publication
Montejo, Victor
White flower : a Maya princess / by Victor Montejo ; illustrated by Rafael Yockteng ; translated by Chloe Catan.
Translation of: Blanca flor.
ISBN 0-88899-599-7
1. Mayas–Juvenile fiction. 2. Yockteng, Rafael II. Catan, Chloe III. Title.
PZ8.1.M65Wh 2005   j863'.64   C2005-901082-7

The illustrations are in watercolor and graphite pencil.
Printed and bound in China

White Flower
A MAYA PRINCESS

VICTOR MONTEJO

ILLUSTRATED BY

RAFAEL YOCKTENG

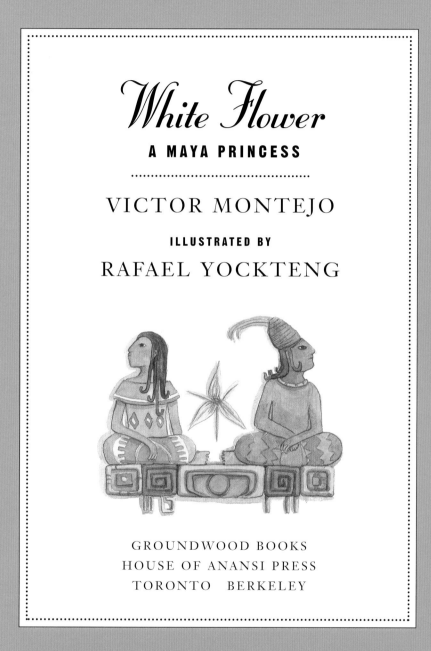

GROUNDWOOD BOOKS
HOUSE OF ANANSI PRESS
TORONTO   BERKELEY

There was once a young prince named Witol Balam, who set out on a journey to look for work in faraway cities and towns. His parents had once been wealthy, but unfortunately the whole country had been swept by an epidemic that killed them and almost everyone else who lived there. The few people who remained were as hungry and poor as the young man. He had suffered so much that he had forgotten who he was. He had even forgotten his own name.

THE YOUNG MAN wandered from place to place, but no one had any work to offer him. One day, tired of walking, he sat beneath a shady tree at the edge of the path. The place was deserted, for hardly anyone walked along that dusty path through the thick forest.

The young man was about to close his eyes and take a nap, when a richly dressed man rode up on a large black deer.

"I can see that you are suffering because you are poor," said the rider. "But I can easily remedy that if you accept my offer."

"What are you proposing, Lord of the Forest?" asked the young man.

"I will give you more riches than you will ever need to enjoy life during your time in this world," the stranger went on. "When you have finished taking pleasure in your wealth, I want you to come and serve me and do whatever I ask of you. But until then you will live like a rich man, with all the money you could wish for."

Like all the people who lived in these Maya towns, the young man knew about Witz Ak'al. He was a strange creature who rode on deer so huge they looked like horses. He brought wealth to those who sought it from him in exchange for their hearts. But when they died, the spirits of these people went straight to Witz Ak'al's mansion, where they were turned into pigs and sacrificed for him to eat.

"Thank you for your offer," replied the young man. "But I cannot accept. My parents taught me to earn my living in an honorable way and never to make deals that could ruin me."

"I am Witz Ak'al, Lord of the Mountains and the Valleys, and I do not bestow my wealth on just anybody. I have chosen you, because I can see how poor you are. Besides, the deal is very simple. After you have had time to enjoy all the pleasures this world has to offer, I will ask you to repay me. All you have to do is accept this money, and you will see how miraculously it grows in your hands. Then you must promise to serve me whenever I need you."

"I may be poor, but I do not want ill-gotten gains," said the young man. "I am strong and hardworking, and I would prefer to

sacrifice myself at hard labor than accept easy money in exchange for my heart."

Seeing that he could not convince the young man, Witz Ak'al rode off angrily.

After resting a while the young man continued on his way. In the distance he could make out a city. The young man approached slowly, asking for the king. People pointed out the way and soon he was at the palace, ready to ask the king for employment.

The king was in the garden with the queen and his beautiful daughter, Princess Saj Haq'b'al, which means White Flower. The young man was amazed to see how much the king resembled the gentleman who had visited him in the forest, offering him riches. Trying to hide his surprise, he bowed before the king, the queen and the princess.

"Good day, my lord, my lady and fair princess," he said.

"Good day, young stranger. What are you doing in these Maya lands?" asked the king in a harsh and unfriendly voice.

"I am looking for work, my lord. I have been walking for many days trying to find a way to earn enough money to rebuild my parents' abandoned house."

The king, who was, of course, Witz Ak'al, remembered how the young man had spurned him and said, "There is no work here, so you might as well be on your way."

The princess, however, who had been listening at the king's side, interrupted. "Father, we need someone like this strong young man to work in the cornfield and look after the bees that provide us with honey and wax for our ceremonies." She pleaded for the young man in such a sweet voice that the king could not refuse.

"Very well, young stranger, I will give you work. I only hope you can do everything I ask," he said, looking at the young man with contempt.

But the young man took no notice and consented to work for the king, the queen and the princess. The king immediately sent him off to a shed behind the palace, where he would stay.

THE YOUNG MAN tried to get some rest, but the king's manner had unsettled him. He was sure that the king was Witz Ak'al, a wicked man who was not to be trusted. Nonetheless, he felt certain that the princess was on his side, and with that thought he fell asleep.

The next day the young man awoke early and went before the king. "My lord, what shall I do today?"

"You must go to the desolate valley for firewood," ordered the king. "Take two large deer with you so you can carry it all back."

That very morning the young man went to the valley. But though he looked everywhere, he found not one piece of wood to chop.

At the end of the day, tired of wandering around with the deer, he went back to the palace empty-handed. He felt bad not to have completed the work the king had asked him to do. And he was afraid that the king would be angry and banish him from the palace.

Timidly, the young man approached the king, who was strolling in the garden.

"Have you brought the firewood?" asked the king.

"No, my lord," replied the young man. "The valley that you sent me to is a desert, and there are no trees. I could not find even one handful."

"That is no concern of mine. If you do not bring me the firewood by tomorrow, you will see what happens to you," threatened the king.

The young man felt miserable. He went back to his shed knowing that he could not carry out the king's orders.

Just then White Flower came to him and asked why he looked so sad. The young man lifted his head and looked at the princess tenderly.

"The king asked me to get firewood, but there is not one single stick of wood to be found in the valley where he sent me. I searched the whole day and found nothing. Now the king has said I must go back to the same place tomorrow. This time I cannot come back empty-handed."

"Poor young man, I understand how you feel," said the princess. I know my father, and he is no ordinary king. He is Witz Ak'al, Lord of the Mountains and the Valleys."

"How can I do what he asks so that he does not punish me?" pleaded the young man.

"You should know that my father does not burn wood in his fires. He uses the bones of dead animals. You should also know that he sometimes turns into a deer, just like other great kings and wise men. My father's animal companion, his *tonal*, is a black deer and my mother's is a brown deer. They are hidden away in a secret garden of the palace. Tomorrow, when you take the deer out to seek firewood, one of them will try to kick you. You must pile a heavy load on his back, for that deer will be my father's *tonal*. The brown deer, on the other hand, must be treated well, since it is my mother's. Everything that happens to these animals will happen to my parents at the same time," explained White Flower.

"Thank you for helping me, lovely Princess," said the young man.

The following day the young man took the two deer and set out for the same place in search of firewood. On the way the black deer he was riding tried to throw him off and kick him. But the young man lashed him with the whip. He soon arrived once more at the parched and barren valley. The land was like a desert, and the deer were perishing from thirst. The bones of dead animals lay in heaps everywhere.

Remembering the princess's words, the young man gathered up the largest bones he could find. Then he made a heavy bundle to tie onto the deer that had tried to kick him. For the brown deer, he made a lighter bundle. And on the way back, every time the black deer tried to kick the young man, he whipped him.

The young man unloaded the deer at the palace and led them to a dark stable where Witz Ak'al had ordered him to leave them. From there the deer would make their way into the secret garden, which only the king and queen could enter.

Then the young man went into the palace to ask the king what his next task might be. Witz Ak'al was furious when he saw him. A servant was putting bandages on his bruised back. Only the king,

the young man and the princess knew that his back had been hurt by the heavy burden carried by the black deer.

Witz Ak'al wanted to punish the young man severely and decided to set an impossible task.

"Early tomorrow morning, you must go and clear all the land in the valley down there and prepare it for planting. If you do not finish tomorrow, you will be punished."

The young man knew he could never do so much work in one day. Unlike the valley of bones, this valley was thickly forested by huge trees that would be very difficult to cut down. He went back to his shed and sat down to brood about the punishment that awaited him.

While he was deep in thought, White Flower came to him again. "And now, why are you so sad?" she asked.

"Your father, the king, has given me an impossible task. He wants me to clear that whole valley and prepare it for planting. It is a job that will take many days. No one man would ever be able to do it."

"Do not worry. You will see that the work is done by midday. In the afternoon, you will be able to relax."

At midnight the princess went to the valley. In the north, she left a white ribbon; in the south, a yellow ribbon; in the west, a red one and in the east, a black one. Lastly, she walked to the center of the valley and tied a green ribbon to a tree. Then the princess hurried back to the palace.

At dawn the young man set off for the valley. When he arrived he was amazed to see that the land he had been ordered to clear was bare. Only a few trees remained so that the bean vines would have a place to climb up among the corn. All the work had been done, as if by magic. The young man spent his day strolling through the newly made field, admiring the colored ribbons still tied around the trees.

When it was time to go back, the young man happily went before Witz Ak'al. "The work is finished, my lord. What shall I do tomorrow?"

"You are completely done?" exclaimed the king.

"Yes, sir, it was easy."

Witz Ak'al began to worry that the young man might know his secrets. No one had ever been able to carry out his orders before. This young man, however, seemed to be making use of his very own magic. Then the king began to suspect the princess, who visited the young man every afternoon after he had finished his work. This made him more furious than ever.

"Tomorrow you will not go anywhere," he said to the young man. "Just fill a pot with water and bring it to the boil. With the boiling water I will skin a pig to make pork crackling."

"Very well," replied the young man. The task sounded very simple.

That afternoon, the young man was lighthearted. He didn't have to think hard, like before, when the king had assigned him impossible tasks. Heating up water was so simple that he had no need to worry. Instead, he went for a walk in the woods hoping to meet White Flower on one of her afternoon strolls. Sure enough, the princess emerged from the woods with her maidens. Slipping away from her companions, she approached the young man.

"What task has my father given you for tomorrow?"

"Something very easy," said the young man. "He told me to put water on to boil so that he can skin a pig and eat it."

"Oh, how unlucky for you!" cried White Flower. "Have you no imagination? The water is to skin you, for tomorrow he will turn you into a pig."

When he heard the princess's words, the young man almost fainted.

"Please, Princess, tell me how to save my life," he asked quickly.

"In this case there is nothing to be done," she said. "If you want to live, you must flee."

"Escape from your father? That is impossible. He will catch up to me in no time."

With her gentle, kind heart, White Flower felt sorry for the young man. In fact, she had fallen in love with him. Resolved to face her father's anger, she said, "Your humility and sincerity have moved me. I will fly with you and protect you. But I want to marry you when we are free and far away from my father."

The young man, who was also in love with the princess, looked at her sadly and began to make excuses.

"But you know I am poor and have nothing to offer you."

"I do not care about that," replied the princess. "What matters now, if we truly love one another, is to fight side by side and save our lives."

THEY PLANNED to wake up early, when the Morning Star rose. Very worried, the young man went to bed. In her room, the princess could not sleep, thinking of how she would have to trick her father to escape.

Toward midnight the princess got up and placed an ear of yellow corn on her headboard. Next she went to the kitchen and placed an ear of white corn on the pile of bones on the hearth. Finally she went outside to the courtyard and placed an ear of red corn by the large door that led to the forest. Then she returned to her bed. No one had seen her.

It was almost three o'clock in the morning when Venus, the Morning Star, appeared in the sky. The time had come. Together White Flower and the young man left the palace, heading down the forest path that led to the Maya kingdoms of the lowlands.

Not long after, Witz Ak'al awoke, and as usual called for the princess. He didn't often call for her so early, but he was suspicious that the princess and the young man were becoming too close.

"White Flower! It is time to get up," he ordered.

"I am getting up," replied the ear of yellow corn that she had left on her headboard.

The king heard White Flower's voice and feeling relieved, went back to sleep. A while later he woke up again and called out, "White Flower, what are you doing?"

"I am in the kitchen lighting a fire," replied the ear of white corn that she had left on the hearth.

Confident that his daughter was in the kitchen, the king fell asleep again. When he awoke for the third time, Witz Ak'al called out to his daughter once more.

"White Flower, what are you doing?"

"I am here in the courtyard, collecting more firewood," answered the ear of red corn that she had left by the main door.

Certain that his daughter was outside working, the king fell asleep once again. Meanwhile, the princess and the young man were hurrying away, farther and farther from the palace.

It was almost daybreak when the king shouted again, "White Flower, what are you doing now?"

No one answered.

Afraid that he had been deceived by his daughter, the king called out, "White Flower, where are you?"

There was no answer. Deep silence lay over the kitchen and the courtyard. Witz Ak'al jumped up and realized that his daughter was nowhere in the palace. He went straight to the young man's shed and saw that he was not there, either. Desperate about his daughter's absence, the king woke up the queen.

"My queen, our daughter White Flower has run away with that young man who came to the palace looking for work!"

"How ridiculous," exclaimed the queen. "Go and catch those young people and bring them back here immediately." The queen was very bossy and she ordered everyone around, even Witz Ak'al.

"I will go at once," said the king.

Realizing that the fugitives must have gained a good head start, the king went down to the secret garden to fetch the black deer. The doors immediately swung open as he came out riding the elegant, swift animal. The deer galloped off at top speed in obedience to the king's command.

MEANWHILE, White Flower and the young man had not slowed their pace. After a couple of hours, the princess said, "I can feel that my father is catching up with us."

"What will we do? Shall we hide?"

"No, he would find us right away. I know how to make him go back to the palace without us," said the princess.

They stopped in the middle of the path. In the distance they could see the dust billowing up from the black deer's hooves. White Flower took a wooden comb that was in her hair. After chanting a few magic words, she threw the comb down onto the path. Instantly a hedge of thorns grew up, blocking the deer's way.

In vain, Witz Ak'al looked for a way through. But seeing that the thorny hedge was impenetrable, he turned around and galloped back.

Sweating and out of breath, the king arrived at the palace and braced himself to tell the queen about his failed quest.

But before he even had time to dismount, the queen demanded, "Have you brought the princess?"

"I could not," said Witz Ak'al. "I was racing along on the deer until I came to a thorn hedge. I couldn't get through."

"Why didn't you bring one of the thorns? That hedge was White Flower herself!"

"How can that be?" asked Witz Ak'al. "I will go back and get one of those thorns right away."

"Go as fast as you can, because I want to see my daughter," insisted the queen.

Once again the king set off from the palace, galloping at full speed on the black deer. He soon reached the spot where the barrier of thorns had blocked his way. But the thorn hedge was no longer there, and the way was clear. So he galloped on, chasing the young man and the princess.

After a few hours the princess felt that her father was drawing near. "My father has almost caught up with us again," she said.

"What shall we do now?" the young man asked, alarmed.

"Don't worry, I know how to make him go back without us," said White Flower.

They could see the deer in the distance. The princess took a small round mirror out of her bag and placed it in the middle of the path. Instantly, the mirror turned into a deep blue lake.

The deer came to a halt when he saw the water at his feet. Remembering the thorns, the king searched for the young people along the shores of the lake but could not find them. Thinking it was a real lake, he turned and went back to the palace.

He was exhausted by the time he arrived.

"Have you brought the princess?" demanded the queen, who was waiting for him in the courtyard.

"The thorn hedge isn't there anymore," said Witz Ak'al. "I went as fast as I could, but my way was then blocked by a deep blue lake."

"You are so foolish, even if you are the lord of the forest!" shouted the queen. "If you wanted to bring our daughter back, you should have collected some of that water, for that water was White Flower."

The king lamented having made such an error. After having a bite to eat, he set out again in search of the fugitives. This time he would bring back the thorns or the water, if he managed to find them.

WITZ AK'AL galloped off on his black deer. The deer ran on and on, swift as the wind, until he came to the spot where the lake had been. But just like the hedge of thorns, the lake had now disappeared. The path ahead was wide and clear, so the deer ran on at top speed.

After many hours of walking, White Flower turned to the young man again and said, "I can feel my father catching up to us once more."

"What will we do to escape him this time?" asked the young man, alarmed.

"Don't worry, I know how to mislead him." The princess untied one of the colored ribbons from her hair and tore one end into seven strips. Carefully, she placed the ribbon on the ground, spreading the strips so that each pointed in a different direction. At once, the seven-pointed ribbon turned into a path with seven branches.

The deer was galloping ahead at full speed, but he stopped when he reached the place where the path divided. The king could not decide which way to take, so he turned around and went back to the palace. He was crestfallen and exhausted.

Just as before, the queen was waiting.

"Have you brought the princess?" she said.

"I could not catch up with them. They must have hidden somewhere. I was closing in on them when I came to a path that branched out in seven directions. I was puzzled and could not decide which one to take," said the king.

"And why didn't you bring back some dust from that path? That seven-branched path was White Flower," replied the queen.

The king could not stand to be scolded any longer. "I am very tired," he said. "Now it is your turn to go and find them and bring them back to the palace."

THE QUEEN went down to the secret garden and fetched the brown deer. She set off at once on the beautiful animal, dashing down the path along which the couple had escaped like a flash of lightning. The deer ran on and on as fast as she could, and very soon the queen had almost caught up with the two fugitives.

The princess began to feel her mother's presence, and she turned to the young man. "We are lost. Now it is my mother who has come, and she is getting very close. And she is almost impossible to fool."

The young man wanted to keep on running, but they were both very tired. So they stopped, and White Flower said, "I will turn into an ear of corn in this big field. You will be the farmer, carefully tending the cornfield. When my mother comes and asks if you

have seen a young couple running away, tell her that the corn is not for sale. You must not let her cut even one ear," said the princess.

Instantly, a cornfield appeared. The cornstalks were thick and green and loaded with tender ears of corn. At the edge of the field an old farmer was tending the plants.

Shortly after, the queen rode up on her deer. She halted in front of the farmer and asked, "Old man, have you seen a young woman and a young man run past?"

Wiping his forehead with his sleeve, the old man replied, "My lady, this corn is not for sale."

When she heard the farmer's answer, the queen guessed immediately that the princess had turned herself into an ear of corn. She got down and walked up to the farmer.

"So the corn is not for sale?" she asked.

"No, my lady, the corn is not for sale," replied the farmer.

The queen quickly walked over to a very fat ear from which long corn silk was dangling. She reached up and grabbed it, saying, "I am sorry, but I cannot go home without one of these splendid things." Then the queen snapped the ear off the plant.

The poor farmer had nothing to say.

WHEN THE QUEEN arrived at the palace with the corn, the young man and White Flower suddenly appeared there, too, as if by magic.

Witz Ak'al was pleased to have his daughter back. He had decided he would be very nice to her from now on, so that she would not run away again. Happily, he said, "You have finally come back home, my daughter. You will stay here while this young man, who tried to kidnap you, will be driven from the palace forever."

The princess disagreed. She was in love with the young man and wanted him to stay at the palace as well. And so in a firm, serious voice she answered, "I do not want you to banish the young man from the palace. I want him to stay here, because I want him to marry me."

"That is not possible," said the king and the queen, taken aback.

"If you do not accept him, we will run away again," White Flower replied.

Seeing that they could not separate the young man and the princess, since the spark of love had already been kindled between them, the king and queen gave in. But if the young man wanted to marry White Flower, he had to do so according to the customs of the place.

THE YOUNG MAN was ordered to go into the forest and cut down a large pile of wood, and then return, carrying it on his back. This would show that he could bear the burden of marriage.

So he went to the forest and chopped a huge stack of wood. He strapped it to his back and walked through the streets of the city so that everyone could see him. Every man had to do this in order to show the bride's parents that he could support a household. The young man arrived at the palace with the large pile of wood, followed by a long line of men carrying smaller piles on their backs.

In the same way, a group of young girls escorted the princess, weaving cloth that they gave to the young men who were following the groom. This was a custom of the Maya people of that region.

The young man had proved that he really could work, and that he deserved White Flower's hand. And so Witz Ak'al pronounced the date of the wedding.

On that day the young man dressed in elegant clothes, and he began to feel like a prince once again. He even remembered his true name, Witol Balam.

So with his heart bursting for joy, Prince Witol Balam married Princess Saj Haq'b'al, or White Flower. The party lasted many days and the musicians played age-old songs on their *marimbas*, so that the people of the city could dance and forget all their sorrows.

It is said that the couple lived many happy years together, raising their children and watching them grow up in that long ago Maya palace.

THE ORIGINS OF "WHITE FLOWER"

"Blanca Flor" or "White Flower" was originally a Spanish folktale. It took many forms once it arrived in the New World. In New Mexico, "Blanca Flor" became a version of "Snow White." In South America, criollos told a version closer to the Spanish original, in which Blanca Flor is instrumental in bringing her suitor through the trials set by her possessive and jealous father.

The author of this book, Victor Montejo, a Jacaltec Maya, was told yet a different version by his grandmother. In this story, the father, W'itz Ak'al, is none other than the Maya demi-god, the Lord of the Forest (*el Señor del Bosque*), combined with a Maya *cacique* or king, who commands both nature and the city. And his daughter, Blanca Flor, is a powerful creature in her own right. She, too, can command the forces of nature.